We Talked in the Tree

An Ivy and Mack story

Written by Juliet Clare Bell

Illustrated by Gustavo Mazali
with Nadene Naude

Collins

Who and what is in this story?

Listen and say

Mum

handstand

Download the audio at www.collins.co.uk/839819

"Quickly, Mack! We're going!" said Ivy.

"I'm reading my comic," said Mack.
"Do you want to see?"

"No, Mack. Come to the park with Luke
and Emma!" said Ivy.

At the park, Luke said, "Look at me!" and he did a handstand.

Mack clapped.

"Can you do that?" Luke asked Ivy.

"Ivy can do everything," said Mack.
"Show Luke," he said to Ivy.

Ivy tried to stand on her hands.
She fell down.

"I'm better at handstands than you," said Luke.

"I can do it," said Ivy. "But I need a tree."

Ivy stood on her hands and put her feet on the tree.

"Hello!" said a girl.

Ivy looked up. There was a girl in the tree. She had long black hair.

"Hello!" said Ivy. "I'm Ivy. What's your name?"

"I'm Mina," said the girl in the tree. "What are you doing?"

Ivy said, "My cousin is better than me at handstands, so I'm trying to get better."

"Who is your cousin?" asked Mina.

Ivy climbed up into the tree. She sat next to Mina. She pointed at Luke. "That's my cousin."

"The tall boy?" asked Mina.

"Yes," said Ivy.

"Who are they?" asked Mina.

"The boy with the long brown hair is my brother, Mack," said Ivy. "He's younger than me. He's five. And the short girl is my cousin, Emma."

"How old are you?" Ivy asked Mina.

"I'm seven," said Mina.

"I'm seven, too," said Ivy. "What school do you go to?"

"We're new here," said Mina. "I start at Gully Road School next week."

"Oh! Mack and I go to Gully Road School! Who is your teacher?" said Ivy.

"Mr Hill," said Mina.

"We're in the same class! We can be friends."

This was exciting for Ivy. It was nice to have a new friend.

"Is that comic *Jump*? My brother reads it every week," said Ivy.

"Oh, me too!" said Mina. "I love comics."

Mina and Ivy read the comic in the tree. It was a lot of fun.

"I need to go home now," said Mina.

"And I need to learn handstands,' said Ivy. "Can you do a handstand, Mina?" Mina did a good handstand.

"Wow!" said Ivy. "That's great!"

"I can teach you," said Mina.

"See you on Monday!" they both said.

Ivy met Luke, Emma and Mack at the playground. They jumped on the roundabout.

"We saw you in the tree, Ivy!" said Luke.

"I was with my new friend, Mina," said Ivy. "We talked in the tree!"

"There's a Mina in my class!" said Mack. "She's tall and she's got short brown hair and glasses. She likes robots."

"That's a different Mina," said Ivy. "This Mina is short. Her hair is black and it's longer than mine. And she's better at handstands than Luke."

"Can I get a comic, please, Mum?"
said Ivy. "Mina and I love comics. We like
to read them in a tree ..."

Picture dictionary

Listen and repeat

black hair

brown hair

glasses

long hair

short hair

tall

short

1 Look and order the story

2 Listen and say

Collins

Published by Collins
An imprint of HarperCollins*Publishers*
Westerhill Road
Bishopbriggs
Glasgow
G64 2QT

HarperCollins*Publishers*
1st Floor, Watermarque Building
Ringsend Road
Dublin 4
Ireland

William Collins' dream of knowledge for all began with the publication of his first book in 1819.

A self-educated mill worker, he not only enriched millions of lives, but also founded a flourishing publishing house. Today, staying true to this spirit, Collins books are packed with inspiration, innovation and practical expertise. They place you at the centre of a world of possibility and give you exactly what you need to explore it.

© HarperCollins*Publishers* Limited 2020

10 9 8 7 6 5 4 3 2

ISBN 978-0-00-839819-4

Collins® and COBUILD® are registered trademarks of HarperCollins*Publishers* Limited

www.collins.co.uk/elt

Author: Juliet Clare Bell
Lead illustrator: Gustavo Mazali (Beehive)
Copy illustrator: Nadene Naude (Beehive)
Series editor: Rebecca Adlard
Publishing manager: Lisa Todd
Product managers: Jennifer Hall and Caroline Green
In-house editor: Alma Puts Keren
Project manager: Emily Hooton
Editor: Deborah Friedland
Proofreaders: Natalie Murray and Michael Lamb
Cover designer: Kevin Robbins
Typesetter: 2Hoots Publishing Services Ltd
Audio produced by id audio, London
Reading guide author: Julie Penn
Production controller: Rachel Weaver
Printed and bound by: GPS Group, Slovenia

Download the audio for this book and a reading guide for parents and teachers at www.collins.co.uk/839819